THE TOP TEN WEIRDEST BUGS

whitestar kids

LET'S GO!

REAL LIFE IS OFTEN STRANGER THAN FICTION! THIS IS ESPECIALLY TRUE WHEN IT COMES TO INSECTS, SOME OF THE MOST NUMEROUS AND DIVERSE LIFE-FORMS ON OUR PLANET.

Generally, insects are so small that they usually go unnoticed. However, some species have such extravagant shapes, unbelievable evolutionary tactics, and explosions of color that you can't help but be amazed. Who's the weirdest? There are many candidates competing for this title, each with its own special features that make it unique...

DISCOVER THEM WITH US AS WE COUNT DOWN TO NUMBER ONE.

BIZARRE FEATURE

FUN FACT

Look for these symbols to discover the surprising **FUN FACTS** and **BIZARRE FEATURES** that earned these **TEN ANIMALS** a spot on our list!

THE WEIRDNESS LEVEL WILL RISE FROM 10 UP TO THE INCREDIBLE NUMBER 1!

At the bottom of the page you will find the names of all **TEN INSECTS**. Try to guess their position in the list by writing each name next to the number you think is correct.
READ THE BOOK TO FIND OUT HOW MANY YOU GOT RIGHT!

1 ______________

2 ______________

3 ______________

4 ______________

5 ______________

6 ______________

7 ______________

8 ______________

9 ______________

10 ______________

- **SCORPION FLY**
- **HERCULES BEETLE**
- **GIRAFFE WEEVIL**
- **WATER STRIDER**
- **ORCHID MANTIS**
- **NUT WEEVIL**
- **HUMMINGBIRD HAWK-MOTH**
- **PICASSO BUG**
- **GLOWWORM**
- **SPINY DEVIL KATYDID**

IDENTIFYING INSECTS

People are quick to shout **BUG**! However, we often assume something is an "insect" when it is actually a completely different animal! Let's get this cleared up before we get started!

INSECTS HAVE SPECIFIC CHARACTERISTICS, STARTING WITH THEIR BODY SHAPE, WHICH IS ALWAYS COMPOSED OF THREE DISTINCT PARTS: HEAD, THORAX, AND ABDOMEN.

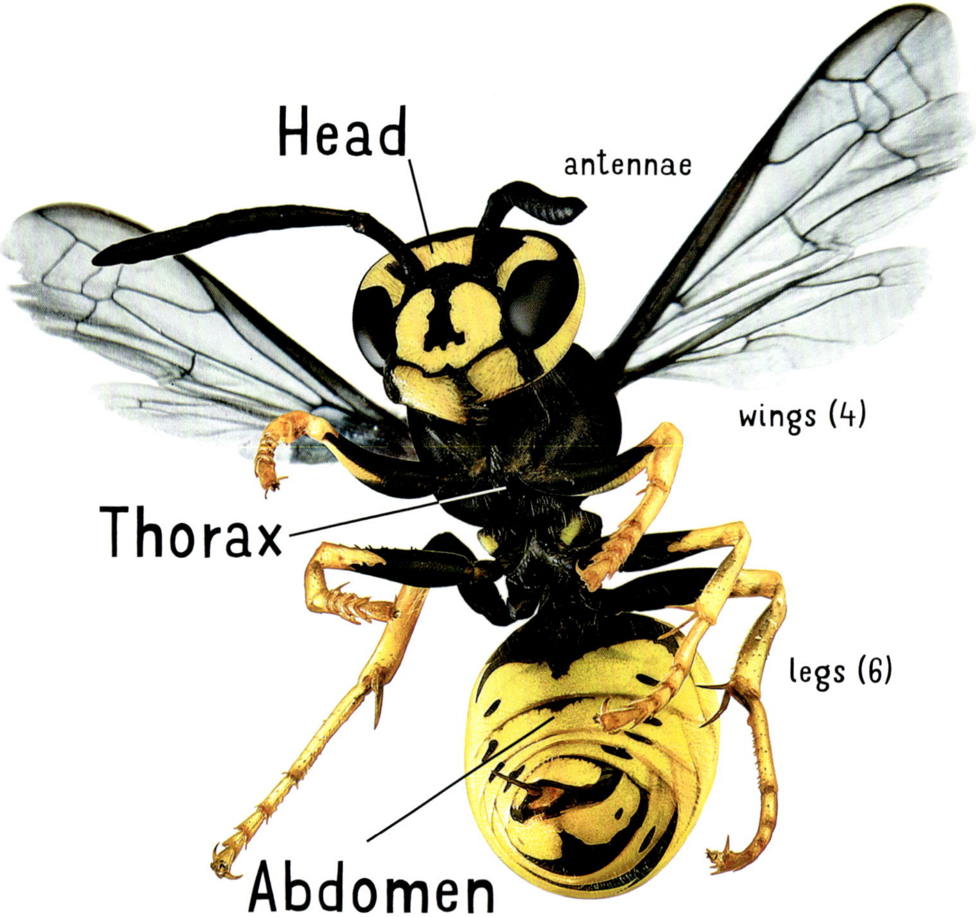

There are **more than 1 million** recognized species of insects, and that number is growing every day.

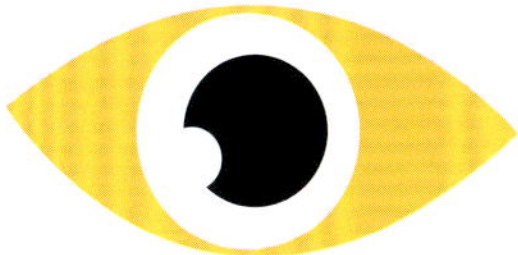

Insects are **arthropods**, and their bodies are covered with an exoskeleton.

Head

The head contains a **MOUTH** as well as other sense organs, such as **OCELLI**, **EYES**, and **ANTENNAE**. The shape of the mouth depends on what the insect eats. The eyes are composed of many **LENSES**, each of which sees a small part of an image.

Thorax

This is the **MIDSECTION** of the body, where we find the appendages responsible for movement: **LEGS** and **WINGS**. There are always **6** legs and **4** wings. In some insects, such as mosquitoes and flies, the second pair of wings is very small and helps them to maneuver better during flight. Beetles, like ladybugs, have a first pair of hardened wings that cover the second pair. Other insects, like fleas, **HAVE NO WINGS AT ALL**.

Abdomen

This last part has no external features, except for small appendages known as **CERCI** or a **STINGER**, such as in the case of bees and wasps.

DON'T CALL US INSECTS!

Arthropods are invertebrate animals with an exoskeleton and articulated legs. All insects are arthropods, but not all arthropods are insects!

SOME ANIMALS BELONG TO THE ARTHROPOD GROUP BUT ARE NOT INSECTS, SUCH AS:

Spiders and scorpions

Unlike insects, **SPIDERS** and **SCORPIONS** are part of the **ARACHNID** family and have eight legs attached to a body composed of only two sections: a cephalothorax and an abdomen. They are also missing antennae and don't have wings.

There are about 60,000 known species of arachnids, of which over 50,000 are spiders.

Millipedes and centipedes

MILLIPEDES and **CENTIPEDES**, such as the **SCOLOPENDRA**, are easily recognized by their very long bodies and incredible number of legs. The former are slow and harmless animals, while the latter are swift predators, mainly of insects, which they immobilize with their venomous bite.

millipedes

Their names (*millipede* means "one thousand feet" and *centipede* means "one hundred feet") do not reflect the actual number of legs they possess, which are far fewer than implied.

scolopendra

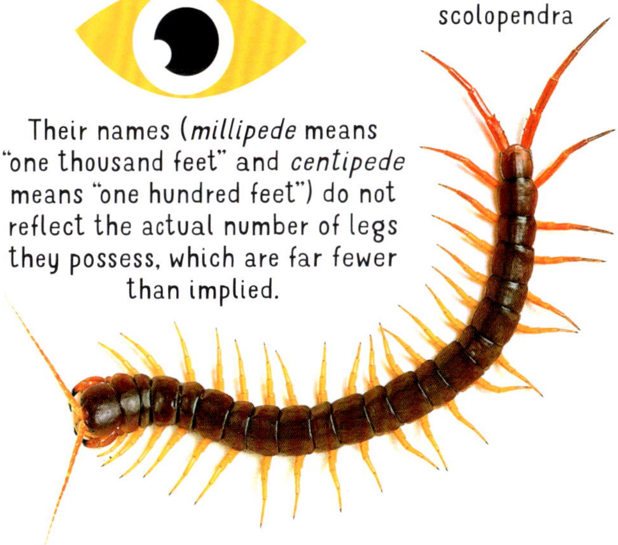

Crustaceans

The last important group of arthropods is **CRUSTACEANS**. It is unlikely that anyone would ever confuse a crab with an insect, but you might have some doubts if, for example, you meet a **PILL BUG**, which, unlike other crustaceans, lives in the wet earth and beneath flower vases.

When frightened, the pill bug will roll up into a ball.

NUMBER

10 GLOWWORM

SCIENTIFIC NAME:
Lampyris noctiluca

SIZE: 1 in (2.5 cm, females), 0.7 in (1.8 cm, males)

To make a **SIGNAL** in the dark, you usually need a light source, don't you? Well, that's exactly what the glow-worm does to draw attention to itself.

The female, who stays on the ground, uses her abdomen to send out intermittent flashes of **BRIGHT YELLOW-GREEN**.

She'll turn on her light for a couple of hours every night until it is noticed by a male flying by, who then uses his own **LIGHT SIGNAL** to answer her call.

DIET:
slugs and snails as larvae; they do not feed as adults

HABITAT:
Europe and northcentral Asia, in fields and at the edges of forests

BIZARRE FEATURE

It uses bioluminescence to search for a partner.

FUN FACT

The female has no wings and looks more like a larva than an adult insect.

NUMBER

9 HERCULES BEETLE

SCIENTIFIC NAME:
Dynastes hercules

SIZE: 7 in (18 cm)

The incredible **STRENGTH** of this insect justifies its name, borrowed from the hero of Greek mythology. According to some scientists, this animal is **THE STRONGEST IN THE WORLD**. It can actually carry items up to 850 times its own weight. Males have two horns, one on the thorax and a longer one on the head, which form a "**PINCER**" that is one and a half times their body length. When fighting with each other, they can open it up to 1.5 inches (4 cm) wide, then close it around their opponent's body and squeeze very hard.

DIET:
very ripe or decomposing fruit

HABITAT:
South America, in rainforests

BIZARRE FEATURE

The long horns of the males and their incredible strength.

FUN FACT

Its abdomen changes color when the air is humid: from yellow or olive green to black.

NUMBER

8 NUT WEEVIL

SCIENTIFIC NAME:
Curculio nucum

SIZE: 0.27 inch (7 mm) without the rostrum

Why does it need such a **STRANGE SNOUT** that is so long and thin? This insect is the sworn enemy of hazelnut plants. With its long, hard proboscis, called a **ROSTRUM**, the weevil sucks the sap out of leaves, making them turn yellow and fall. Females use their rostrum to drill holes through the hazelnut shell. They lay their eggs inside, one for each nut. This will be the birthplace of the **LARVA**, who then eats the nutritious flesh of the nut to grow and mature.

DIET:
hazelnuts as larvae; hazelnut leaves as adults

HABITAT:
Europe and North America, in forests of hazelnut trees

BIZARRE FEATURE

The thin rostrum of the female is as long as her whole body.

FUN FACT

Its body is covered with thick hairs that are the same color as ripe hazelnuts.

NUMBER

7 PICASSO BUG

SCIENTIFIC NAME:
Sphaerocoris annulus

SIZE: 0.4 in (10 mm)

This insect looks like it came out of an abstract painting by an artist with an overactive imagination.
Why is it so dressed up?
The incredible patterns of color are actually a **WARNING SIGN** to ward off anyone with bad intentions. They announce that this animal, like many other shield bugs, is extremely **SMELLY** and it would be best to stay away. If the assailant does not withdraw, the bug falls to the ground and **PLAYS DEAD**.

DIET:
flowers and leaves of various plants

HABITAT:
Africa,
in tropical savannas

BIZARRE FEATURE

Stunning designs and bright colors decorate the body.

FUN FACT

They suck the nectar and sap of many plants by piercing them with a small pointed proboscis.

AS BEAUTIFUL AS JEWELS!

Insects often make people react with disgust. Some, however, have developed such striking colors that they resemble precious jewels or miniature works of art.

ALL IT TAKES IS A FEW GEOMETRIC LINES, SYMMETRICAL PATTERNS, AND BRIGHT COLORS TO MAKE US ADMIRE THESE LITTLE ANIMALS. HERE ARE SOME OF THE MOST BEAUTIFUL INSECTS:

Jewel beetles and wasps

The **SHIMMERING** colors of jewel beetles and jewel wasps are simply impossible to ignore! They shine in the sunlight, emitting metallic **REFLECTIONS** in shades of emerald green, gold, red, and blue.

Some cultures use the wings of jewel beetles to make earrings.

The colors are iridescent, meaning they change if you view them from different angles.

jewel wasp

Owl butterfly

Only when the owl butterfly opens its wings can we see its intricate design, with spots, wavy lines, and stripes that alternate between light and dark colors. Doesn't this look like the work of a skilled artist?

The two large spots on the wings mimic the eyes of an owl.

Thanks to its colors, this butterfly can easily hide on the bark of trees.

Caterpillars

Butterflies are beautiful, but their larvae are often even more so! Queen butterfly caterpillars, for example, have a royal appearance with their black and white striped dress and yellow patches. Spurge hawk-moth caterpillars are also elegant, thanks to their striped design and white spots.

spurge hawk-moth caterpillar

Their vivid coloring helps them pretend to be poisonous.

In addition to color, sometimes even hairs give caterpillars an incredible appearance!

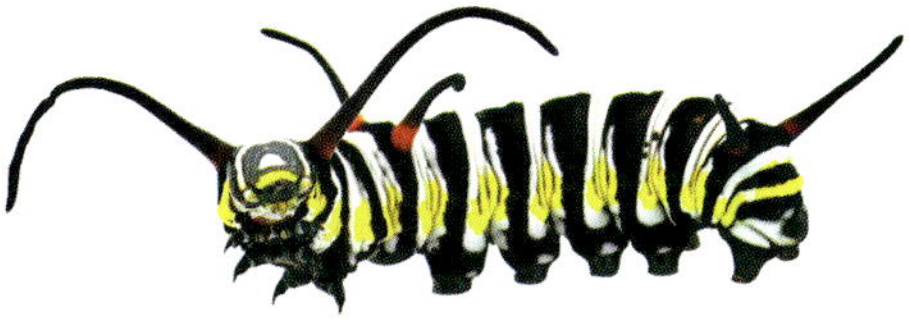

queen butterfly caterpillar

NUMBER

6 SCORPION FLY

SCIENTIFIC NAME:
Panorpa communis

You can't help but be afraid! Have you seen my stinger?

SIZE: 1.1 in (3 cm)

This bug is a big **FAKE**! At the bottom of the abdomen, we see a tail ending with a **POINTY TIP** that the animal curls upward. This position makes it look exactly like the venomous **STINGER** that all scorpions have. In truth, it is nothing more than a **TOTALLY HARMLESS** appendage, present only in males, and used exclusively during reproduction, for courting and holding on to their mate.

DIET:
nectar, fruit, dead insects

HABITAT:
Europe, North America, and North Asia, in hedges and wooded areas

BIZARRE FEATURE
The curved tail looks like a scorpion's stinger.

FUN FACT
It often steals leftover food from spider webs.

NUMBER

5 SPINY DEVIL KATYDID

SCIENTIFIC NAME:
Panacanthus cuspidatus

SIZE: 3 in (7.5 cm)

At first glance, the spiny devil katydid might look a bit silly. However, it is actually a **CUNNING HUNTER** that captures other insects by **AMBUSHING** them.

Using its long, spiny front legs, it grabs them in a quick, precise strike. If necessary, its **ARMED LEGS** are also useful for self-defense. The **SPINES** scattered across its body give it a pretty monstrous appearance, but most importantly, they make it an uncomfortable snack for predators.

DIET:
small insects

HABITAT:
South America, in rainforests

BIZARRE FEATURE

Spiny armor and a red crown with three points on its head.

FUN FACT

Its bite is powerful enough to cut through human skin.

NUMBER

4 ORCHID MANTIS

SCIENTIFIC NAME:
Hymenopus coronatus

SIZE:
2.4 in (6 cm, females),
0.78 in (2 cm, males)

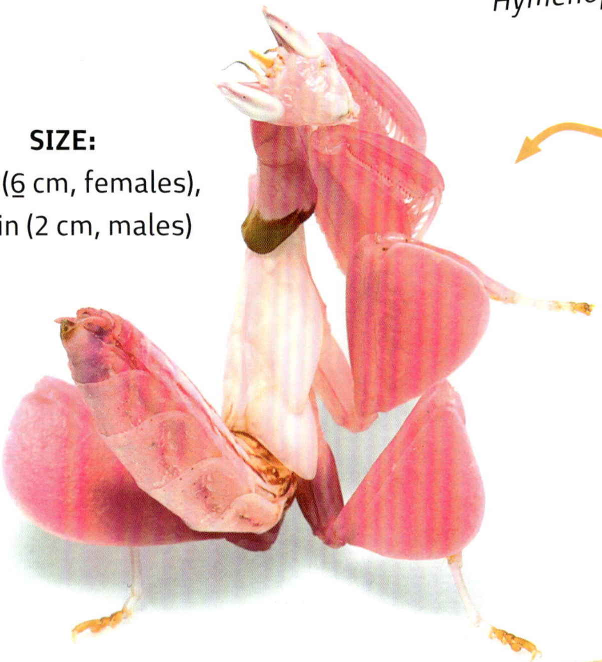

This insect is just as **BEAUTIFUL** as it is **DANGEROUS**. It actually disguises itself as a flower to lure in unsuspecting insects. When the moment to attack arrives, it grabs its prey with one **LIGHTNING-FAST STRIKE** of its toothed front legs and quickly turns it into dinner. In addition to looking like a flower, the orchid mantis also acts like one: it attaches itself to a twig and swings back and forth, as if swaying in a light breeze. Some scientists think that the floral dress is also the perfect disguise for hiding from predators.

DIET:
small arthropods, especially pollinators

HABITAT:
Southeast Asia, in rainforests

BIZARRE FEATURE
Body parts that resemble flower petals.

FUN FACT
According to some scientists, the orchid mantis attracts more bees than real flowers do.

THE ART OF DISGUISE

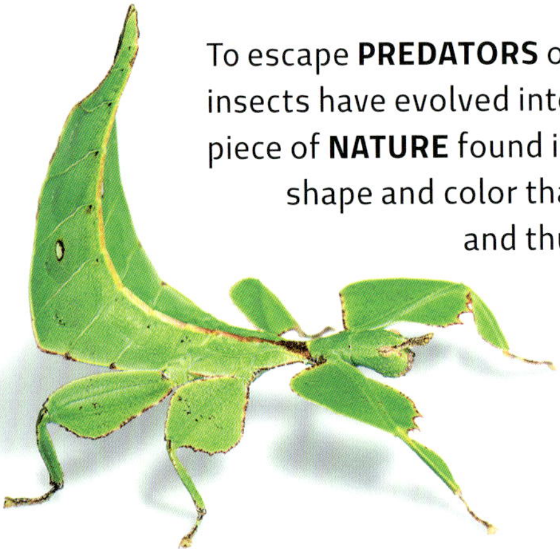

To escape **PREDATORS** or **TRICK** unsuspecting prey, many insects have evolved into mimics, meaning they imitate a piece of **NATURE** found in the environment so perfectly in shape and color that they blend in with the real thing and thus avoid detection.

A VERY CLEVER TOOL FOR BOTH PREY AND PREDATOR, DON'T YOU THINK?

How to look like a leaf

That leaf has eyes! Of course it does because it's actually an insect dressed in **CAMOUFLAGE**. Imitating the appearance of a leaf, whether it's a vibrant green or a dry brown, is quite popular among insects. When hanging from a twig, a **DEAD LEAF BUTTERFLY,** a **DRY LEAF INSECT,** or a **GREEN LEAF INSECT** is virtually impossible to spot.

They are surprisingly good at copying the jagged edges, veins, and colors of a leaf!

How to look like a twig or thorn

STICK INSECTS are phantom insects. With their incredibly long, thin bodies and matching legs, they are easily confused with twigs in a tree. They can be as long as 8 inches (20 cm). If a predator grabs one of their legs, **IT BREAKS OFF** and regrows with the next shedding of the **EXOSKELETON**.

Meanwhile, **THORN INSECTS** position themselves along a branch and make the plant they rest upon appear full of prickly spikes, which discourages predators from catching them.

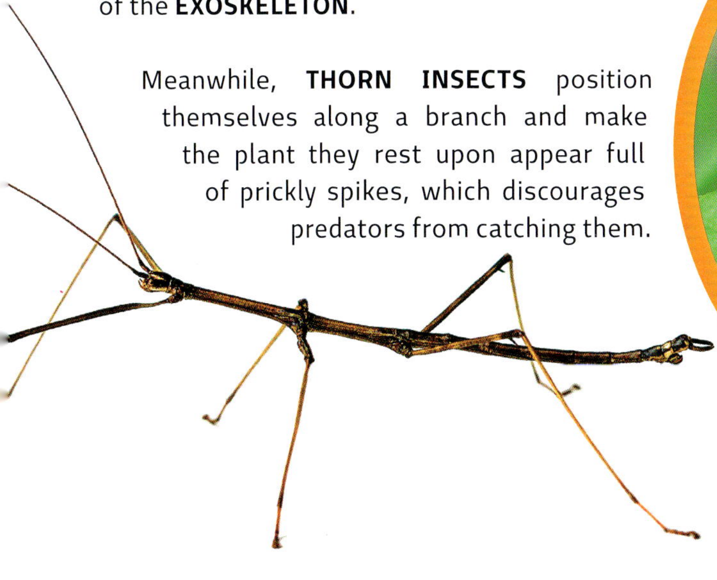

THE ART OF STANDING OUT

Some insects, such as ladybugs and bees, want to be highly visible, which is why they have striking colors like **RED**, **ORANGE**, and **YELLOW**. This is how they warn everyone that they are **POISONOUS** or **TASTE DISGUSTING**. Their message is clear: "Stay away from me because I am not good to eat and can seriously hurt you!"

OTHER INSECTS HAVE COME UP WITH THEIR OWN CLEVER TRICK, IN WHICH THEY DEVELOP AN INCREDIBLE RESEMBLANCE TO THEIR POISONOUS COUSINS. THEY HAVE NO UNPLEASANT OR DANGEROUS CHARACTERISTICS, BUT IT'S VERY USEFUL TO MAKE PREDATORS THINK THEY DO! HERE ARE THREE EXAMPLES:

Viceroy butterfly

Viceroy butterflies imitate monarch butterflies to protect themselves from birds. Indeed, birds avoid monarch butterflies because they are **POISONOUS**.

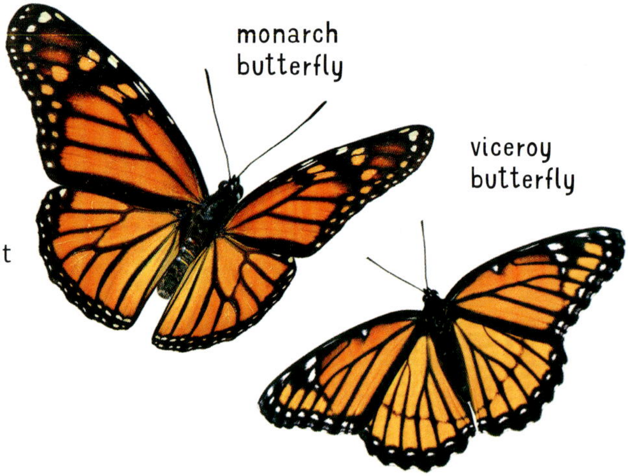

Hoverflies

Another clever disguise is used by the hoverfly, a defenseless **FLY** whose abdomen is striped yellow and black just like a wasp.

hoverfly

wasp

hoverfly

Swallowtail butterfly caterpillar

If you can imitate a dangerous predator, then you can inspire true **FEAR** in your attackers. At first glance, the small swallowtail butterfly caterpillar looks like a **SNAKE**. It has fake eyes on one end of its body to trick predators.

The markings perfectly imitate the features of a snake.

NUMBER

3 WATER STRIDER

SCIENTIFIC NAME:
Gerris lacustris

SIZE: 0.6 in (1.5 cm)

Many people dream of being able to walk on water. The water strider does this with ease, using 4 of its 6 legs to glide across the surface of a pond as if it were ice skating. Why doesn't it sink? Thanks to two different features!
First of all, its legs trap **SMALL AIR BUBBLES** that work like **LIFE RAFTS**. Additionally, they are covered with short hairs coated with a waterproof wax that makes them "float."

DIET:
small animals, dead or alive

HABITAT:
Europe, North America, and Asia, on bodies of still water

BIZARRE FEATURE

Long, thin feet that skate across the water's surface.

FUN FACT

They can move quite fast, reaching a speed of 33 miles per hour (15 meters per second).

UNUSUAL BEHAVIOR

The water strider isn't the only insect with qualities that seem unusual to humans.

INSECTS ARE OFTEN BIZARRE ANIMALS, NOT ONLY IN APPEARANCE BUT ALSO IN HOW THEY BEHAVE. HERE ARE A FEW EXAMPLES:

Walking in single file

PINE PROCESSIONARY CATERPILLARS move in single file, forming a line that can become several yards long! Given their great number, they are among the most destructive **PARASITES** in the world. Hundreds of these caterpillars can strip entire trees, devouring almost all the pine needles in a forest.

Their hairs cause irritation when they come in contact with skin, as well as when they are inhaled.

Farming mushrooms

LEAFCUTTER ANTS walk back and forth along the same path every day to cut fragments of leaves from plants within a 100-yard radius. Then, holding the pieces firmly with their **JAWS**, they carry them back to the ant nest.

The leaves are then used as nourishment for mushrooms that are "farmed" by the ants in a special section of the nest, similar to a vegetable garden.

Going on migration

We know that many birds migrate with the changing seasons. However, not everyone knows that many insects do it too. Among the more adventurous travelers we find the **MONARCH BUTTERFLY**. Every autumn, thousands of them leave the cold lands of **NORTH AMERICA** and fly 2,500 miles (4,000 km) to reach the forests of **MEXICO** for the winter.

NUMBER

2 GIRAFFE WEEVIL

SCIENTIFIC NAME:
Trachelophorus giraffa

I'm not the cuddly type!

SIZE: 3.5 in (9 cm, males), 2 in (5 cm, females)

The most extraordinary feature of the giraffe weevil is, obviously, its incredibly long **NECK**, which is almost three times longer for the males than it is for the females. The antennae are right at the tip and are used during battle to win the attention of a mate. When fighting, each male sits on a leaf and starts hitting the opponent's neck in an attempt to knock him down. The long neck is also used for building a **NEST** to protect young **LARVAE**.

DIET:
leaves ... like the mammal it's named after!

HABITAT:
the forests of Madagascar

BIZARRE FEATURE
Extremely long neck in males.

FUN FACT
When frightened, they play dead and stay still for an hour.

NUMBER

1

HUMMINGBIRD HAWK-MOTH

SCIENTIFIC NAME:
Macroglossum stellatarum

You didn't confuse me with a tiny bird, did you?

SIZE: 2.2 in (5.5 cm)

At first glance, it isn't easy to distinguish this large **MOTH** from the bird of similar name and size, the **HUMMINGBIRD**! Like the bird, this moth approaches flowers to suck nectar while flapping its wings very quickly. It inserts a very long **PROBOSCIS** into petals with tube-shaped corollae, remaining **SUSPENDED IN FLIGHT** for the time necessary to feed on the **SWEET NECTAR**. Unlike other moths, the hummingbird hawk-moth is active during **DAYLIGHT** hours, from dawn to dusk.

DIET:
nectar from flowers

HABITAT:
Europe, Asia, and North Africa, in forests and meadows

BIZARRE FEATURE

A long proboscis and flight with rapid wing beats.

FUN FACT

They can flap their wings 70–80 times a second, emitting a vibrating hum.

BIZARRE QUESTIONS

TRY TO ANSWER THESE QUESTIONS, WITHOUT WORRYING ABOUT MISTAKES! TURN THE PAGE TO SEE THE CORRECT ANSWERS!

1- HOW LONG DOES AN ADULT GLOWWORM LIVE?

A 2 weeks

B 2 months

C 2 years

2- WHAT DOES THE HERCULES BEETLE EAT?

A Other insects

B Flowers and leaves

C Fruit

3- WHERE DO NUT WEEVIL LARVAE SPEND THE WINTER?

A Inside a hazelnut

B Below ground

C Under tree bark

4- WHAT TYPE OF METAMORPHOSIS DO PICASSO BUGS GO THROUGH?

A Complete

B Incomplete

C None

5- WHICH FLYING FACT ABOUT SCORPION FLIES IS TRUE?

A They fly very high

B They don't fly

C They rarely fly

6- WHERE DO YOU FIND THE HEARING ORGANS ON A SPINY DEVIL KATYDID?

A On the legs

B On the mouth

C On the wings

7- WHAT SURPRISING THING DOES THE MANTIS ORCHID SOMETIMES DO?

A It gives off a scent

B It changes color

C It walks on its antennae

8- WHAT'S ANOTHER NAME FOR WATER STRIDERS?

A Pond giraffes

B Moses bugs

C Water spiders

9- WHAT DO GIRAFFE WEEVILS USE TO BUILD THEIR NESTS?

A Leaves

B Mud

C Bark

10- WHY ARE HAWK-MOTHS ALSO KNOWN AS SPHINX MOTHS?

A Because of their larvae

B In honor of the person who discovered them

C Due to their Egyptian origins

BIZARRE ANSWERS

1, A

Adults live only long enough to reproduce. Larvae, on the other hand, grow for two or three years before fully maturing.

2, C

While their larvae feed on decomposing wood, the adults eat rotten fruit that has fallen to the ground.

3, B

With the arrival of autumn, the nut weevil larva leaves its hazelnut and falls to the ground, where it enters the pupa stage. It will emerge as an adult in the spring.

4, B

These insects, unlike butterflies, already have a very adult-like appearance when they first hatch from their eggs, differing in only a few small details such as color and the absence of wings.

5, C

Although they do have wings, scorpion flies prefer to move around in the damp earth, walking among the leaves.

6, A

Like all members of the katydid family, the spiny devil katydid hears very well, thanks to the hearing organs located on the second segment of its two front legs.

7, B

When it notices something new in its environment, the orchid mantis can slowly change color from light pink to dark brown.

8, C

Like spiders, water striders prey on other insects. Another fact: their mouth has evolved into a hollow straw, called a rostrum, that is suitable for piercing and sucking.

9, A

The nest is made from a carefully rolled leaf, in which the female deposits a single egg.

10, A

When frightened or irritated, the larva of this insect raises the front of its body and adopts a position that looks like the ancient Egyptian Sphinx.

CRISTINA BANFI

Since graduating in Natural Sciences from the University of Milan, she has taught in various schools. For more than 20 years, she has worked in scientific communication and educational play and has enjoyed several editorial experiences in both scholastic and educational fields, particularly those dedicated to a young audience. In recent years she has created several titles for White Star.

PHOTOGRAPHIC CREDITS

A. Kehinde/Shutterstock: 14; Agsaz/Shutterstock: 30; Alslutsky/Shutterstock: 5 bottom; Art789/Shutterstock: 2, 8; Attentive Simia/Shutterstock: 24 center; Butterfly Hunter/Shutterstock: 26 bottom left, 31 bottom left; CHAIYARAT/Shutterstock: 3 top; Cynoclub/Shutterstock: 24 bottom; D'animulls Chase/Shutterstock: cover top right, 1 top right, 17 bottom, 27 top left; Dayusasono Rhonny/Shutterstock: 19; Deer Tom/Shutterstock: 20; Dileepa Photo/Shutterstock: cover center; Dracaena Ana/Shutterstock: 21; Fawver Melinda/Shutterstock: 25 bottom; George photo cm/Shutterstock: cover top left, 16 top; Grimplet/Shutterstock: 1 top left, 5 center; Gstalker/Shutterstock: 12; GUDKOV ANDREY/Shutterstock: 31 bottom right; Hamilton Stuart/Shutterstock: 7 bottom; Hauke Tobias/Shutterstock: 6 top; HHelene/Shutterstock: cover center, 32; Imageman/Shutterstock: back cover bottom left, 3 center; Irin-k/Shutterstock: back cover top,1 bottom right, 26 top, 26 center, 40 left; Isselee Eric/Shutterstock: 17 center, 25 top; Janicki Sebastian/Shutterstock: 16 bottom; Jiaranaisakul Kawin/Shutterstock: cover bottom left, 1 bottom left, 22; Keifer Cathy/Shutterstock: 26 bottom right; Khlungcenter/Shutterstock: 6 bottom, 9; Kozyrev Anton/Shutterstock: 27 top right, 27 top center; Kuttelvaserova Stuchelova/Shutterstock: 35; Lasenby Brian/Shutterstock: 27 bottom; leaw7824/Shutterstock: 7 top left; Matee Nuserm/Shutterstock: 24 top, 40 right; Miko Jan/Shutterstock: 29; Minihane Chris/GettyImages: 15; Nechaevkon/Shutterstock: 18; Petr Lerch/Shutterstock: back cover bottom right, 3 bottom; Pisut chounyoo/Shutterstock: cover bottom right, 10; Pong Wira/Shutterstock: 23; Posteriori/Shutterstock: 4; Prezzemoli Beatrice/Shutterstock: 28; Protasov AN/Shutterstock: 5 top, 36 left top, 36 left center, 36 left bottom, 36 top right, 37 top, 37 center, 37 bottom, 5 top; Puttachat Kumkrong/Shutterstock: 7 top right; Rodri75/Shutterstock: 25 center; Skonieczny Andre/GettyImages: 13; Sumit sanit/Shutterstock: 11; Super Prin/Shutterstock: 17 top; van de Water Dennis/Shutterstock: 33; Vieru Danut/Shutterstock: 34; Wells Kevin Photography/Shutterstock: 31 top; Wirestock Creators/Shutterstock: 16 center.

Editorial Coordination
Giada Francia

Design and layout
Valentina Figus

Piazzale Luigi Cadorna, 6 - 20123 Milan, Italy
www.whitestar.it

Translation: Qontent
Editing: Michele Suchomel-Casey

First printing, May 2024

ISBN 978-88-544-2099-1
1 2 3 4 5 6 28 27 26 25 24

Printed and manufactured in China
by XY Cultural and Creative Park, Guangzhou

MIX
Paper from responsible sources
FSC® C178000